MAIN

W9-CCM-106

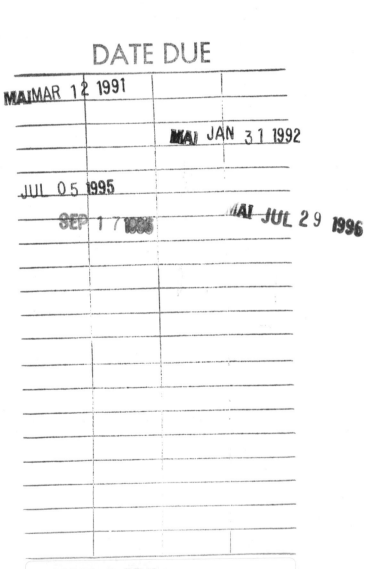

HOW THE GUINEA FOWL GOT HER SPOTS

How the Guinea Fowl Got Her Spots

a *Swahili tale of friendship*

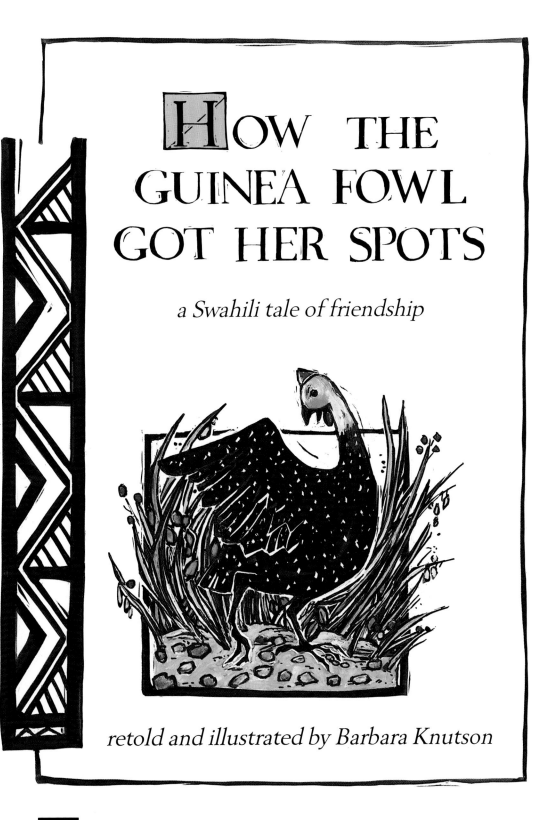

retold and illustrated by Barbara Knutson

Carolrhoda Books, Inc./Minneapolis

The name *Nganga* is pronounced
n'GAHN-gah.

Library of Congress Cataloging-in-Publication Data

Knutson, Barbara.
    How the guinea fowl got her spots : a Swahili tale of friendship / retold and
illustrated by Barbara Knutson.
       p.   cm.
    Summary: A folk explanation for the guinea fowl's protective
coloration that enables it to hide from its natural predator, the
lion.
    ISBN 0-87614-416-4 (lib. bdg.)
    [1. Folklore—Africa. 2. Guineafowl—Folklore.] I. Title
PZ8.1.K728Ho   1990
398.24′528618′096—dc20
[E]   89-25191
                                        CIP
                                        AC

Manufactured in the United States of America

1 2 3 4 5 6 7 8 9 10 99 98 97 96 95 94 93 92 91 90

To the Cecilwood friends

A long time ago,
when everything had just been made,
Nganga the Guinea Fowl had
glossy black feathers all over.
She had no white speckles
as she does today—
not a single spot.

Guinea Fowl was a little bird,
but she had a big friend.
And that was Cow.

They liked to go to the great green hills where Cow could eat grass and Nganga could scratch for seeds and crunch grasshoppers.

And they would both keep an eye out for Lion.

One day, Guinea Fowl was crossing the
river to meet Cow on the most delicious
hill they knew. The grass was so juicy
and thick that, even from the river,
Nganga could hear Cow hungrily
tearing up one mouthful
after another.

But...

what was that
Nganga saw
slinking toward Cow?

Was it ...?
Yes, it was LION!

Now you might think a guinea fowl is
no match for a lion, but Nganga didn't
think that. In fact, she didn't think at all.
She scratched and scrambled up
the bank as fast as she could
and whirred right
between Cow and Lion,
kicking and flapping
in the dust.

"RAAUGH!" shouted Lion.

"My eyes! This sand! What was that?"

When the clouds of dust thinned there was no sign of anyone— certainly not any dinner for Lion. He went home in a terrible temper, growling like his empty belly.

The next day, Guinea Fowl was at the grassy patch first. You can be sure she had her eyes wide open for Lion.

Soon she saw Cow cautiously crossing the river to join her— shlip, clop, shlop. But something yellow was twitching in the reeds. Wasn't that Lion's tail?

Up whirred Nganga, half tumbling,
half flying with her stubby wings.
Lion looked up, startled,
from his hiding place.
Frrrr… a little black whirlwind
was racing across the grass
toward the river.
"Whe-klo-klo-klo!"
it called out to Cow.

Guinea Fowl! That's where the duststorm came from yesterday," growled Lion between his sharp teeth. But the next moment, the whirlwind hit the river.

"RAAUghmf!" Lion exploded with a roar that ended underwater.

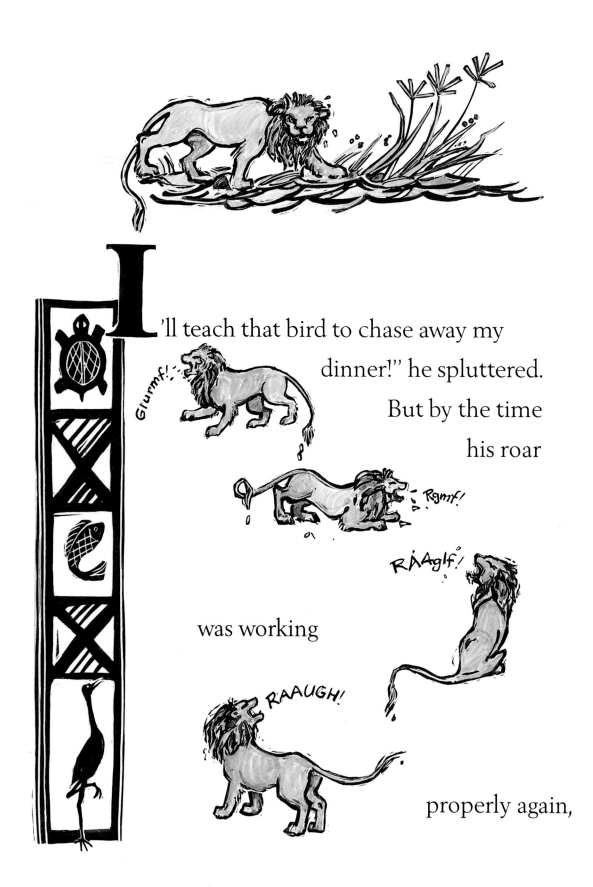

I'll teach that bird to chase away my dinner!" he spluttered. But by the time his roar

Glurmf!

Rgmf!

RÅAglf!

was working

RAAUGH!

properly again,

Cow and Guinea Fowl
were safely over the next
hill at Cow's house.

N ganga," mooed Cow gratefully, "twice you have helped me escape from Lion. Now I will help you do the same."

Turning around, she dipped her tasseled tail into a calabash of milk. Then she shook the tasselful of milk over Guinea Fowl's sleek black feathers— flick, flock, flick—spattering her with creamy white milk.

Guinea Fowl craned her head
and admired the delicate speckles
covering her back.

She spread her wings,

and Cow sprinkled them with milk too—
flick, flock, flick.

W he-klo-klo!
That's beautiful, Cow!"
chuckled Nganga.
"Thank you, my friend!"
And she set off for home.

Whom should she meet
where the path crossed the river
but Lion, still shaking
the water out of his ears
and angrier than ever.

Ho, Speckled Bird!"
snorted Lion.

"Have you seen Guinea Fowl
on your path?"

O h yes," clucked Nganga, hiding a smile.
"I believe she went that way."
She pointed with her spotted wing
to the hills far down the river.
"If you go quickly and don't stop
to rest, you may catch up with her
in a few days."

L

Lion leaped up at once,
not bothering to thank the strange bird.

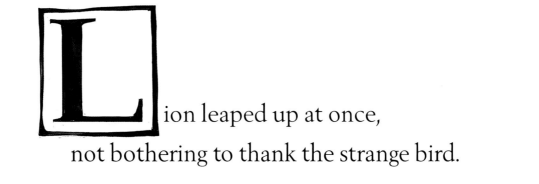

A minute later, he thought
about taking her along for a
traveling snack, but when he looked
back at the riverbank, he could see no trace of her.

"These lovely spots are just the thing for hiding in the shadows and grass!" laughed Nganga, who was, in fact, right where Lion had left her.

And she turned back
to Cow's house
to thank her friend
again.

AUTHOR'S NOTE

Creation stories all over Africa tell how certain animals developed the characteristics that set them apart from others. This story came from East Africa but spread in other versions to other parts of Africa as folktales tend to do.

I used watercolor and India ink on Essdee scratch-board for the pictures in this book. The scratching process corresponds with traditional African design sources, which were often originally scratched into wood, gourds, or metal.